Betsy and Billy

Also by Carolyn Haywood

Betsy and Billy

CAROLYN HAYWOOD

Illustrated by the author

An Odyssey Classic
Harcourt Brace Jovanovich, Publishers
San Diego   New York   London

HBJ

Requests for permission to make copies of any part of the work should be mailed to:
Copyrights and Permissions Department, Harcourt Brace Jovanovich, Publishers,
Orlando, Florida 32887.

Library of Congress Cataloging-in-Publication Data
Haywood, Carolyn, 1898–
Betsy and Billy/written and illustrated by Carolyn Haywood.
p.   cm.
"An Odyssey classic."
Summary: Betsy, Billy, and their friends enjoy and learn from
the many activities in the second grade.
ISBN 0-15-206768-X (pbk.)
[1. Schools—Fiction.]   I. Title.
[PZ7.H31496Be   1990]
[Fic]—dc20   89-39894

Printed in the United States of America
A B C D E

*To my mother
who taught and loved little children
this book is lovingly dedicated*

CONTENTS

Betsy and Billy

1

Betsy Goes Back to School

It was September and vacation days were almost over. Soon it would be time for Betsy to go back to school. She had tried on all of her school dresses that she had worn the year before. Betsy had grown so tall that Mother had to let down all of the hems.

One day Mother was busy hanging the skirt of one of Betsy's dresses. Betsy was standing on a chair. She turned very slowly while Mother put the pins in the skirt.

"Betsy, what are you looking so sober about?" asked Mother.

"I was thinking," replied Betsy.

"And what were you thinking about?" asked Mother.

"I was thinking about school," answered Betsy. "Do you know, Mother, I don't know whether I am going to like being in the second grade."

"Of course you are going to like being in the second grade," said Mother.

"But, Mother, Miss Grey won't be there," said Betsy. "Miss Grey was such a nice teacher. I don't think I am going to like my new teacher. Her name is Miss Little. She isn't pretty like Miss Grey."

"Well, dear, everyone can't be as pretty as Miss Grey," said Mother.

"But Miss Little wears black dresses all the time, Mother," said Betsy. "I used to see her last year and she always had on a black dress. I don't like black dresses. Miss Grey wears pretty dresses, pink ones and green ones and red ones, and once she had a dress that had flowers all over it."

"It has been a long time since school closed," said Mother; "perhaps Miss Little has bought herself some new clothes."

"Well, I hope so," said Betsy.

"Run along now," said Mother, as she helped Betsy down from the chair.

Betsy ran along, but she kept thinking about Miss Little. She began to feel sorry that she had been promoted. *Perhaps I could go back to the first grade*, she thought. But she knew that she wouldn't like that either because she wouldn't know anyone in the first grade. All of her friends were in the second grade. There was her best friend, Ellen, and there was Billy Porter. Betsy chuckled when she thought of Billy. He was such a funny little boy, always calling out from his seat and getting into trouble. Then there were Kenny Roberts and Betty Jane and Mary Lou and the twins, Richard and Henry. She would be so glad to see them all. She would even be glad to see Christopher who sometimes pulled her braids. Betsy could see that she could never give up being in the second grade. She would have to be in Miss Little's room and put up with the black dresses. *Perhaps she hasn't any money to buy pretty dresses*, thought Betsy. And then she began to feel very sorry for Miss Little because she didn't have any money to buy pretty dresses.

One afternoon, Mother cleaned out her closets. She had decided to give away all of her old dresses that she did not wear any longer. At the end of the afternoon she had a big pile of dresses on the bed. She decided to give them to Milly, the laundress. When Betsy saw the pile of dresses, she said, "Mother, may I have some of these dresses to play 'Dress-up Lady'?"

"I think you may," said Mother.

"Oh, Mother," cried Betsy, "may I have this flowered one?" Betsy picked up a flowered silk dress that had been her favorite dress of Mother's.

"Yes," said Mother, "and you may have the red one with the long train. You will be a very grand lady in that dress."

Betsy carried her new treasures off to her own room. She tried them on and paraded up and down the hall. Every few minutes she stopped to look in the mirror. This was a lovely new game and for several days she wore Mother's old dresses almost all of the time. When Ellen came to play with her they each put on one of the

dresses. They played that they lived in separate corners of the playroom and they paid calls on each other, and talked about their children.

The day before school was to open, Betsy was wearing the red silk dress. All of a sudden, she thought of Miss Little and her black dresses. Then Betsy had an idea. She took off the red dress and laid it on the bed. Then she pulled the flowered silk one out of the bottom drawer of her bureau. She looked at them very carefully. They were a little mussed and a little soiled around the bottom, but Betsy thought they really looked very nice. She tried to smooth out the wrinkles and all the time she had wrinkles in her forehead, for it was very hard to decide which dress she could part with. She loved them both very much, but she had decided to give one of the dresses to Miss Little. First she thought she would give her the flowered one, but she ended by thinking the red one would be best. Miss Little would look nice in the long train. Betsy folded the dress as carefully as she could and put it in her schoolbag.

The next morning, just as she was leaving for school, Mother said, "Betsy, whatever is in your schoolbag that makes it look so fat?"

"Oh, that is your red dress," replied Betsy.

"I am going to give it to Miss Little so that she will have a pretty dress to wear to school."

"Betsy, darling!" cried Mother. "You can't give that dress to Miss Little."

"Why not?" asked Betsy, looking very crestfallen. "It's a present for her."

"You can't give dresses to your teacher, dear," explained Mother. "You can give her flowers or candy or fruit and many other things, but not dresses."

Betsy looked puzzled but she opened her schoolbag and pulled out the dress. Mother hugged her little girl very tight when she kissed her good-bye.

Betsy trotted off to school thinking it was very strange that dresses couldn't be presents. Soon she met some of her little friends. They chattered about their summer vacations all the way to school.

When they reached the big wide street, there was Mr. Kilpatrick, the policeman. When he saw the group of children, he blew his whistle and all of the automobiles stopped. The children ran toward the big policeman, calling, "Hello, Mr. Kilpatrick."

Mr. Kilpatrick laughed and shouted, "Hello, there, everybody! Hello, Billy. How are you, Teddy? Why, there's Little Red Ribbons!" Mr. Kilpatrick always called Betsy "Little Red Ribbons" because she often wore red ribbons on her braids.

The children swarmed around the policeman. "Mr. Kilpatrick," shouted Betsy, "I can milk a cow!"

"You don't say so!" said Mr. Kilpatrick.

"Our cat has kittens, Mr. Kilpatrick," said Teddy.

"Look, Mr. Kilpatrick," cried Billy, "I have a loose tooth."

"Run along, run along," shouted Mr. Kilpatrick, as he hustled the children on.

When the children reached the school they trooped into the second-grade room. To Betsy's surprise, Miss Little wasn't there. Instead, the school secretary was standing at the front of the room. "Just take your seats quietly, children," she said. "Your teacher will be here in a few minutes. Miss Little is not coming back to school."

Betsy wondered who her teacher would be. She saw Miss Grey pass the door. She was so glad to see Miss Grey again. It was all she could do to keep from running after her. She began again to wish that she could go back to the first grade with Miss Grey. Betsy could feel a little lump in her throat. She swallowed hard but it didn't do any good. Just as the tears were beginning to come into her eyes, the door opened and in came Miss Grey. "Good morning, boys and girls," said Miss Grey.

"Good morning, Miss Grey," the children said.

"I have a surprise for you," said Miss Grey.

The children's eyes were very wide, for they loved nothing better than surprises.

"I have been promoted," said Miss Grey. "I am in the second grade, too."

"Whoopee!" shouted Billy Porter.

2

What Happened to Billy's Tooth

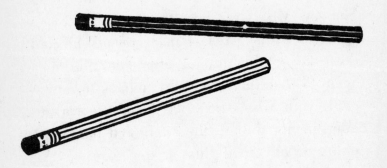

B illy Porter was very proud of his loose tooth. No one else in the second grade had a loose tooth so of course this made Billy feel very important indeed. At recess he stood in the center of a circle of friends and wiggled the tooth.

Betsy thought Billy's loose tooth was wonderful. When she came home from school she said, "Mother, Billy Porter has a loose tooth. Will I have a loose tooth too pretty soon?"

"I suppose you will, Betsy," replied Mother. "Your baby teeth should be coming out soon."

"Will all of my teeth come out?" asked Betsy.

"Yes," answered Mother, "but new ones will come in to take their places."

Each day Billy's tooth grew looser and every day his little friends gathered round him to see how loose it was.

Betsy could hardly wait for the day to come when she would have a loose tooth. Every morning, as soon as she woke up, she sat up in bed and felt each of her teeth. One morning when she felt her front teeth, one of them seemed to rock ever so little. Her eyes grew round with

wonder. She felt it again. Yes, she was certain that it moved a tiny bit. Betsy leaped out of bed and rushed into Mother's room. "Mother, Mother!" she cried. "My tooth is loose. Look, Mother, it's loose!"

Mother felt Betsy's little tooth. "Yes, I believe it is," she said.

"Look! Father, look!" cried Betsy. "My tooth is loose!" Father had to stop shaving to look at Betsy's tooth.

"Well, isn't that something!" said Father. "I wonder if any of mine are loose."

Betsy laughed at Father while he felt his front teeth, for Betsy knew that none of Father's teeth were loose. They were big and white and strong.

Then Betsy's face fell. "Oh, dear," she sighed.

"What's the matter?" said Father, as he went on shaving.

"I just remembered," said Betsy. "Today is Saturday and I don't go to school today. Now I'll have to wait until Monday to show everybody."

"Cheer up!" said Father. "It will be looser by Monday. You'll be able to get a bigger crowd around you on Monday."

Betsy went back to her room a little comforted. While she dressed she thought of Billy Porter.

He wasn't the only one with a loose tooth now. How would she ever be able to wait until Monday, she thought. And there was Sunday in between too.

Betsy found that waiting until Monday was not as bad as she had thought. On Saturday morning the grocer's boy came with the groceries. The milkman came to collect his money for the milk. The gas man came to look at the gas meter and a man came selling brooms. As each one arrived, Betsy said, "I have a loose tooth."

Betsy thought that the grocer's boy and the gas man and the man selling brooms didn't act as though they thought a loose tooth was very important, but the milkman thought it was wonderful. When she told him about her tooth, he said, "Now that's the best news I've heard all morning. Sure it will be a great day when it comes out."

On Monday morning the tooth was looser. It really wiggled. Betsy reached school very early. She showed it to Miss Grey and to all of the children as they came into the room. When Billy Porter arrived the children were crowded around Betsy. "Oh, Billy!" they shouted. "Betsy has a loose tooth too."

"Well, mine will come out first," said Billy, "because mine is looser than yours."

"Maybe it won't," said Betsy, " 'cause mine is pretty loose."

"There's not a chance," said Billy, "not a chance."

When the bell rang for school to begin the children sat down in their seats.

"Children," said Miss Grey, "I am going to give a brand-new red pencil to the first one who loses a tooth." Miss Grey had red pencils and green pencils, but the red pencils were very special and were always used as first prizes.

Billy pointed to himself and grinned. "That means me," he said.

At recess time no one gathered around to look at Billy's tooth. Now that there were two loose teeth in the second grade, Billy's didn't seem so important.

Betsy was letting Ellen feel hers when Billy came up to her.

"You think you're smart, don't you," said Billy, "getting a loose tooth. Well, you're just a copy-cat."

Billy was so cross that he shoved Betsy very hard. "You old copycat!" he cried.

Now Betsy had been standing on one foot, and when Billy shoved her she toppled over and her little nose struck the hard cement of the school yard.

When Billy saw what he had done, he was so scared that he ran away as fast as he could.

Ellen helped Betsy up. Betsy was crying and there was a little blood on her lip.

The bell had already rung for the children to return to their classrooms. Ellen put her arm around Betsy. When Miss Grey saw Betsy crying, she said, "Why, Betsy, what has happened?"

"Billy Porter knocked her down," said Ellen.

"I didn't mean to knock her down," said Billy. "I just gave her a push and she upset."

"Billy, I am ashamed of you," said Miss Grey. "I want you to apologize to Betsy and tell her you are sorry."

Betsy had stopped crying. The tears were still wet on her cheeks but she was smiling a big broad smile. Before Billy could say he was sorry, Betsy called out, "Oh, Miss Grey, I've lost my tooth."

Miss Grey handed Betsy a new red pencil. "Now, Billy," said Miss Grey, "we are waiting to hear you tell Betsy that you are sorry you knocked her down."

"I'm sorry I knocked you down," murmured Billy.

"Oh, that's all right," said Betsy, looking at her new red pencil. "I'm not sorry; I'm glad."

Then a strange look came over Billy's face. His eyes were big and round and he looked scared.

"What's the matter, Billy?" asked Miss Grey.

"I swallowed it," said Billy.

"What did you swallow?" asked Miss Grey.

"My tooth," said Billy.

"Thank goodness!" said Miss Grey. "Now we

are rid of those teeth." Then she looked at the class. "How many children think that Billy should have a green pencil?"

All of the children raised their hands.

"Thank you," said Billy, as he took the pencil. In a few moments Billy raised his hand.

"What is it, Billy?" asked Miss Grey.

"That tooth won't bite me, will it, Miss Grey?" said Billy.

The children laughed very hard at Billy's question.

"No, Billy," said Miss Grey, "it won't bite you."

3

The Halloween Party

All during the month of October, the children in the second grade were looking forward to Halloween. They could hardly wait for the last day of October to come. One day Miss Grey told them that they could have a Halloween party on that day.

"Can we come to school dressed up?" Kenny Roberts asked.

"Well, you can't come to school dressed up," Miss Grey replied, "but you can bring your costumes with you and put them on at lunchtime and we will have a party."

"Will there be ice cream?" said Billy. "It won't be a party if there isn't any ice cream."

"I don't know about ice cream," said Miss Grey. "We shall have to see when the time comes."

When Ellen went to Betsy's house to play, they talked about what they would wear. In the schoolyard they whispered about it because they wanted to surprise the other children. Everybody wanted to surprise everybody else but everybody whispered to somebody about what he was going to wear.

As the day drew near, funny false-faces appeared in the store windows. There were clowns and Indians, monkeys and donkeys, rabbits and cats. There were old men with great big noses and ladies with bright pink cheeks and fuzzy hair.

At last the day came. Betsy woke up with a happy, "special-day feeling." She knew that this was going to be a day full of fun. She was going to be the Queen of Hearts. Mother had made a long blue dress for Betsy. It was very stiff and there were big red hearts fastened all over it. There was a crown for Betsy to wear on her head. It was made of cardboard and painted with gold paint. When it was time for Betsy to leave for school, Mother folded the dress very carefully and put it in Betsy's schoolbag.

Betsy trotted off with her schoolbag over her shoulder and her crown hanging on her arm. When she reached the corner, she turned around and ran home. "Mother," she shouted, "I forgot the pillow that goes under my dress to make me look fat."

Mother gave Betsy an old sofa pillow and Betsy started off again. This time her arms were full. On her way to school she met some of the other children. They were all carrying brightly colored clothes in their arms or packages done up in brown paper. Some of the children were wearing their false-faces. They laughed and shouted. Suddenly it began to rain. The children ran as fast as their legs could carry them. They didn't want their Halloween costumes to get wet. When they reached the school, Kenny Roberts stopped at the drinking fountain to get a drink of water, but everyone else ran right into the classroom.

"Now, children," said Miss Grey, "I want you

to put all of the costumes and the false-faces under the desks. We will keep them there until lunchtime."

After a while Kenny came in. He had his false-face in his hand and he was crying.

"What's the matter, Kenny?" asked Miss Grey.

"I lost my Halloween suit," said Kenny.

"But how did you lose it?" said Miss Grey.

"I don't know," sobbed Kenny. "I had it when I left the house and now I haven't got it."

"You must have dropped it," said Miss Grey. "Go look in the schoolyard."

Kenny went out in the yard. It was pouring now. Soon he returned carrying a very wet suit. "I guess I dropped it when I stopped to get a drink," he said.

Miss Grey took the suit from Kenny and hung it over the radiator to dry. Betsy thought it looked just like her winter night-drawers only it was dark gray and there was a long tail hanging from the seat of the trousers.

"I know what that is," said Ellen. "It's a pussycat suit."

Soon steam began to rise from the pussycat suit.

"Miss Grey," said Kenny, "do you think it will be dry in time for the party?"

"Yes, Kenny," replied Miss Grey, "we'll leave it there all morning and it will be dry and warm when you put it on."

When the lunch bell rang, Miss Grey told the children to take out their costumes and put them

on. In a moment the room was buzzing. The children were busy putting on skirts and jackets, trousers and boots, hats and scarves. The false-faces were on in a jiffy.

Kenny took his suit off the radiator. What was his surprise when he found that it was so tiny he couldn't begin to put it on. "What is the matter with my suit?" cried Kenny. "I can't get it on."

"Oh, Kenny!" said Miss Grey. "It must have shrunk. Isn't that too bad!"

All of the children stopped dressing to look at Kenny's suit.

"That isn't a pussycat suit," said Billy. "It's a kitten suit."

Kenny began to cry for now he had no Halloween suit.

"Don't cry, Kenny," said Miss Grey. "I'll find something for you to wear."

Miss Grey went out of the room while the children finished putting on their costumes. When they were through, the room was full of cowboys and pirates, policemen and firemen. There were Gypsies and dancers, Dutch girls and boys in wooden shoes, fairies and elves. Ellen was a Spanish dancer and she had a tambourine that

jingled. Betty Jane was Red Riding Hood and Christopher was a soldier with a sword in his belt.

When Miss Grey returned, she was carrying a brown blanket with bright red stripes. "Here, Kenny," she said. "You can be an Indian."

Kenny stopped crying when he saw the blanket. He looked much happier. Miss Grey wrapped the blanket around him and fastened it with a big safety pin. Then she found some old feathers in her desk drawer. These she fastened to Kenny's head with a rubber band.

When the children were all dressed, they came up to the front of the room, one by one. Each child told the others what he was supposed to be. The children clapped for every one. When Betsy said that she was the Queen of Hearts, they clapped very hard. Finally, it was Kenny's turn. He walked to the front of the room in his Indian blanket. When he turned round, he was wearing his pussycat false-face. The children laughed and laughed when they saw how funny Kenny looked.

"Well, Kenny," said Miss Grey, "tell us what you are."

"I'm an Indian pussycat," said Kenny.

The children clapped louder than ever and Miss Grey laughed very hard.

"Now," said Miss Grey, "let's have a parade around the room before we eat our lunch." The children formed a line around the room. Betsy's pillow was slipping down so she shoved it up around her middle. Christopher was right behind her rattling his sword. Miss Grey sat down at the piano and began to play a march. The children marched around the room. Betsy was having a hard time with her pillow. It kept slipping down and she kept pushing it up. Suddenly it dropped on the floor. Betsy stepped over it but the soldier with the tin sword tripped and fell on the pillow. Christopher scrambled to his feet and Betsy picked up her pillow. Out flew the feathers all over the room. Christopher's tin sword had cut the pillow cover.

"Oh! Oh!" shouted the children.

The music stopped and Miss Grey turned round. "Gracious goodness!" she cried; "where did this snowstorm come from?"

Just then a boy from the sixth grade opened the door. As he did so, the draught from the open door sent the feathers flying higher than ever. How the children shouted!

When the feathers dropped, they settled all over the room. The children had to gather them up very carefully and put them in a big paper bag.

At last they were all caught and the children settled down to eat their lunch. Miss Grey had a brick of ice cream for each little boy and girl. The children's eyes danced as she put the ice cream in front of them.

"Oh, boy!" cried Billy. "This is a real party all right!"

Just as the children were beginning to eat their ice cream, Kenny said, "Guess what, Miss Grey!"

"I couldn't guess, Kenny," said Miss Grey. "You will have to tell me."

"There's a feather sticking right up out of my ice cream," said Kenny.

4

Bread and Molasses

On Saturday mornings Betsy played with her little friends. Sometimes she went to Ellen's house and sometimes to Billy Porter's. Sometimes Ellen or Billy came to play at Betsy's.

Billy had a new puppy dog. The dog had been named Miss Mopsie-Upsie Tail because her tail stuck up so straight. Most of the time she was called Mopsie for short because nobody could go out front and call, "Here, Miss Mopsie-Upsie Tail! Here, Miss Mopsie-Upsie Tail!" Billy had a lot of different ways of calling her. Sometimes he shouted, "Here, Mopsie-Upsie-Opsie" and sometimes he would call, "Here, Upsie-Opsie-Mopsie" and sometimes, "Here, Opsie-Mopsie-Upsie," so that Miss Mopsie-Upsie Tail soon learned to run home whenever she heard anything shouted with a lot of p's in it.

One Saturday morning Mother drove into the city. She dropped Betsy off at Billy's house. Billy's mother had invited Betsy to spend the whole day with Billy. Betsy had her paintbox with her, for she and Billy had decided to color pictures in a new painting book. They both liked to paint, and whenever they painted pictures that pleased them very much they would climb up three flights of stairs to the top floor of Billy's house to show their work to Billy's father. Billy's father was an artist and he worked all day painting pictures in his studio away up on the top floor.

About ten o'clock Billy's mother looked into the living room. The two children were lying on the floor painting. Mopsie was lying as close to the children as she could. She was almost on top of the painting book.

"I am going to the store now," said Billy's mother. "Don't disturb Daddy because he is very busy this morning."

"Can we have something to eat?" asked Billy.

"Yes," replied his mother. "I left some crackers for you on the kitchen table."

Mrs. Porter went off and the two children ran out to the kitchen. They finished off the crackers in no time.

"Say!" said Billy, "we have some dandy molasses. Do you like bread and molasses, Betsy?"

"You bet!" said Betsy.

"Well, I'll see if I can find it," said Billy.

Billy looked in the refrigerator but the molasses was not there. Finally up on a high shelf he spied a jar filled with golden molasses. Billy climbed up on a chair and reached for the jar. He couldn't quite reach it. Betsy and Mopsie

stood by, looking up at Billy. Billy stood on his toes and stretched up as high as he could. Now he could touch the jar. He moved it with his finger to the edge of the shelf. Now he could get his hand around it. Very carefully he lifted the jar down.

"Oh, boy!" said Billy, as he placed the jar on the table; "I was afraid I was going to drop it."

"I was holding my breath," said Betsy.

Billy took the lid off of the jar. "Now we'll get some bread," said Billy, opening the bread box.

Mopsie had her two front paws against the edge of the table. She didn't want to miss anything, especially not anything to eat.

"Here's the bread," said Billy, handing the loaf to Betsy.

As Betsy reached for the loaf of bread, her elbow knocked against the jar of molasses. Over it went, pouring the golden syrup over the edge of the table right onto Mopsie. In a moment the molasses was all over Mopsie's back.

"Now look what you did," shouted Billy. "What will my mother say!"

Betsy stood the jar up and looked at the sticky mess. Then she looked at Mopsie. The molasses that had fallen on Mopsie's head was now running down over her face. The rest was settling into Mopsie's fur coat.

"Have you got a rag?" asked Betsy. "I'll wipe it up."

Billy gave Betsy the dishcloth and Betsy wiped the molasses off of the table. Then she wiped up all that had gotten on the floor.

"Now you will have to wipe Mopsie," said Billy.

Betsy reached for the little dog, but Mopsie thought Betsy wanted to play so she turned and ran. Through the kitchen door she flew. Round and round the dining room table she dashed. The children ran after her shouting, "Here, Mopsie! Come here!"

Mopsie was having a good time. This was more fun than watching the children color picture books. She flew out into the hall and up the stairs. The children raced after her. Mopsie dashed into Mrs. Porter's bedroom and jumped right into the center of the bed. To Betsy's horror, Mopsie rolled all over the clean white bedspread. Before Billy could pick the little dog up, the bedspread was ruined. There were sticky yellow spots all over it.

Billy clutched Mopsie tightly in his arms. "We'll have to give her a bath," said Billy. "She's sticky all over.

Billy carried the dog into the bathroom. "Turn on the water," he said.

Betsy put the stopper in the tub and turned on the water. She let it run until the tub was half full. Then Billy put Mopsie into the water and the two children set to work. Betsy held Mopsie while Billy washed her. He rubbed soap-flakes all over Mopsie until she was covered with lather. Then he rinsed the soap suds off with clear water. As he lifted the dog out of the tub, Billy knocked against the towel rack. Down went the guest towels into the water.

"Gee!" said Billy; "now look what I did!"

Billy set Mopsie down on the floor and leaned over to pick up the wet towels. Like a flash, Mopsie was off again. Back to the bedroom she scampered leaving wet tracks behind her. The children ran shrieking after her, but before they could catch her she was up on Mrs. Porter's bed again, rolling on the molasses-spotted bedspread. Billy caught her and carried her back to the bathroom. Once again he put Mopsie in the tub and rinsed her off. "Now you hold her," he said to Betsy when he lifted Mopsie out.

Betsy held her while Billy rubbed Mopsie with his own towel. Then he carried her down to the kitchen and put her in her bed. "Now you stay there," he said, "and behave yourself."

When Billy came upstairs again, Betsy said, "What will your mother say about the bedspread?"

Billy looked at the bedspread. It was certainly a sorry sight. "Maybe we better wash it," said Billy.

"Maybe we better," said Betsy.

The children took the bedspread off of the bed and carried it into the bathroom. They put it in the tub and added more soapflakes. They both rubbed it as hard as they could. When they

thought that it was clean, they tried to lift it out of the water but the water made it so heavy they couldn't lift the bedspread.

By this time Billy and Betsy were soaking wet. Betsy's dress was sticking to her and water was dropping off the bottom of Billy's shorts. Betsy's braids had gone into the water so many times that her whole head felt wet. Once more they tried to lift the spread but it was no use. They were not strong enough.

"Perhaps we could lift it if we got into the tub," said Betsy.

"All right," said Billy. The children took off their shoes and stockings and stepped into the tub. Again they tried to lift the heavy spread. They found that they could each lift one end; but no matter how hard they pulled, they couldn't lift the spread out of the tub.

"Now heave," shouted Billy. Betsy heaved. Billy heaved so hard that he sat down in the tub. This upset Betsy and she went down with a splash.

"Daddy!" cried Billy, at the top of his voice. "Daddy, Daddy, Daddy!"

Mr. Porter came down the stairs three steps at a time. When he reached the bathroom door, the two children were standing up in the tub. They looked like drowned rats.

"What's going on?" said Mr. Porter.

"Come help us, Daddy," said Billy. "Come help us."

Mr. Porter squeezed the water out of the children's clothes. Then he helped them out of the tub. Meanwhile Billy and Betsy told him what had happened.

"Betsy, you will have to take off your clothes and put on some of Billy's dry clothes," said Mr. Porter.

Billy trotted off to his own room to change his

clothes and his father got some clothes for Betsy to put on. While the children were dressing, he wrung the water out of the bedspread, the guest towels, and the children's clothes. Then he washed out Billy's towel that Billy had used to dry Mopsie.

When Billy's mother came home, Mr. Porter was hanging Billy's towel on the clothesline.

Mrs. Porter looked at the clothesline. She opened her mouth in surprise. There were the bedspread, the guest towels, all of Billy's clothes, and all of Betsy's clothes. In the doorway stood Billy and Betsy dressed like little brothers.

"What happened?" said Billy's mother.

"I just wanted to give Betsy a piece of bread and molasses," said Billy.

"Well, everything is on the line but the dog," said Billy's daddy.

5

The Present That Betsy Wanted

O ne day in December Mother took Betsy into
the big city. Betsy loved to go to the city,
especially when Mother took her on the train.

On this particular day Betsy was delighted
because Mother was taking her to see the Christmas toys and to buy her Christmas presents.
Betsy had her own money in her little pocketbook.

When they got off the train, Betsy and her mother walked along a wide street. The street was crowded with people. Betsy thought she had never seen so many people before. Everyone seemed to be in a great hurry.

When they came to the corner, Betsy saw a man dressed as Santa Claus. He was ringing a bell and he had a little iron kettle on a stand beside him. Betsy saw a little boy stop and put something in the kettle.

"Mother," said Betsy, "why is the Santa Claus man ringing a bell?"

"He is collecting money to buy Christmas dinners for all of the poor children in the city," replied Mother.

"Can I put some money in the little kettle?" asked Betsy.

"Yes," answered Mother, as she opened her pocketbook.

"Oh, no!" said Betsy. "I want to put my own money in."

"Very well!" replied Mother.

Betsy opened her pocketbook and took out ten cents. When she dropped it in the kettle, the Santa Claus man said, "Thank you, little girl, and a Merry Christmas to you."

Betsy said, "Merry Christmas to you, too," and hurried along with Mother.

Soon they reached a great big department store. Inside of the store there were Christmas trees everywhere. They were all hung with stars that twinkled.

Betsy and Mother walked into an elevator and it shot right up to the top floor. When they stepped out of the elevator, Betsy knew that she was in Toy-Land. She didn't know which way to look first. She could hear music, like the music of a merry-go-round.

"Oh, Mother!" cried Betsy, "there are Jack and Jill and the Three Little Pigs!" Betsy pointed to the top of one of the big posts that held up the roof of the store. Sure enough, there they were, moving slowly around the post.

"And there is Old Mother Hubbard and Tom, Tom the Piper's Son," said Betsy, pointing to another post. Betsy walked around, looking at all of the posts. All of the nursery rhyme people were there, going round and round.

Betsy and Mother looked at all kinds of toys, at games and dollhouses, trains and tricycles, sleds and doll coaches. Betsy saw many toys that she told Mother she would love to have for

Christmas. Each time Mother said, "Well, we'll see."

At last they came to the big glass case that was filled with beautiful dolls. There were big dolls and little dolls, baby dolls and lady dolls. There were little boys and little girls. There were dolls with light yellow curls and dolls with soft brown hair. Betsy thought that all of the dolls in the world must be here. She wandered around and around the glass case. After a while Betsy said, "Mother, I don't want a make-believe baby for Christmas. Do you know what I want, Mother?"

Mother made no reply. Betsy looked up. Mother wasn't there. Betsy looked all around her. Mother was nowhere to be seen. There were a great many people but not one of them was Mother. Betsy stood very still. At first she felt terribly frightened, but then she remembered that Mother had told her that if she ever became separated from her, she should stand very still and wait. No matter how long it seemed, she must not take a step because Mother would always come back for her.

Betsy leaned her little back against the nearest post and waited. She felt surrounded with trouser legs and skirts. They were all walking this way and that way. Ladies' pocketbooks knocked against her head as they pushed past her. Men carrying packages bumped against her hat.

After a while a pair of bright red legs with high black boots came along. Betsy looked up and there, looking down at her, was another Santa Claus. "Well, little girl," he said, "are you lost?"

"No, I'm not lost," replied Betsy, "but I'm afraid my mother is."

"Well," said Santa Claus, "suppose I lift you up and perhaps you will see her. We can't have any lost mothers in Toy-Land."

Santa Claus lifted Betsy up in his big strong arms. Now she could see over everyone's head. There was Mother coming towards her! When Mother reached her, Betsy said, "I stood still, Mother; I stood still and I wasn't scared." Mother patted Betsy's hand.

"And now," said Santa Claus, as he put Betsy down, "tell me what you want for Christmas."

"Well," said Betsy, "I want something very special."

"Very special?" said Santa Claus.

"Yes," said Betsy, "I want a baby."

"You mean a doll-baby that says 'Mamma' and opens and shuts its eyes?" asked Santa Claus.

"No," said Betsy; "a real one that I can have for a baby sister."

"Gracious me!" said Santa Claus. "That's a rather large order, but we'll see about it."

"I would like to have a bicycle too," said Betsy. "But if I can't have both, I want the baby sister."

"I'll make a note of that," said Santa Claus.

Betsy took hold of Mother's hand. As they walked towards the elevator, she said, "Do you think I will get a baby sister for Christmas, Mother?"

"Well, we'll see," said Mother. "Would a baby brother do just as well?"

"Not quite as well," said Betsy; "but it would be better than none."

After Betsy had bought a flashlight for Father and a hair ribbon for Ellen and some handkerchiefs for her granddaddy, Mother said, "I think you had better buy some handkerchiefs for Mrs. Beckett. She is coming to spend Christmas with us."

Mrs. Beckett had been Betsy's nurse when she was a baby and Betsy loved Mrs. Beckett

very much indeed. Betsy picked out two pretty handkerchiefs for Mrs. Beckett. One was pink and the other one was blue.

"Father is going with me to buy your present, Mother," said Betsy. "It's a secret. I'll tell you this much, though. It's something to wear on your hands."

"Oh, my!" said Mother. "Is it a ring?"

"No," replied Betsy. "It's something that covers your hands all up, but I'm not going to tell you because it's a secret."

"Something that covers my hands all up?" said Mother. "Well now, what could that be?"

"It's going to be a surprise," said Betsy, laughing.

Betsy held her presents on her lap in the train. She was very quiet. After a while she said, "Mother, why are there so many Santa Clauses?"

"You see," said Mother, "Santa Claus is the love that makes everyone want to give presents."

"I see," said Betsy. "So there are a lot of Santa Clauses because there is a lot of love."

"Exactly," replied Mother.

A few days before Christmas Mrs. Beckett arrived. Betsy was so glad to see her.

"Do you know what I want for Christmas, Mrs. Beckett?" said Betsy.

"No, I don't believe I do," said Mrs. Beckett.

"I want a baby sister," said Betsy. "Do you think I will get a baby sister, Mrs. Beckett?"

"Well," said Mrs. Beckett, "we'll see."

"That is what Mother says," replied Betsy.

At last Christmas Eve arrived. Betsy went to bed early so that Christmas morning would come sooner. Mother heard her say her prayers and tucked her into bed.

"Mother," said Betsy, as she held her very tight, "do you think I will get a baby sister?"

"I'm not sure," said Mother, as she kissed her little girl.

Soon Betsy fell fast asleep. It seemed like no time at all when she was awake again. Betsy knew that it was morning because she could see a little bit of light in the sky. Just then Mrs. Beckett tiptoed into the room. She was dressed in a stiff white dress and she was wearing white shoes.

"Can I get up now?" whispered Betsy.

"Yes," said Mrs. Beckett. "Come and see the present that Mother has for you."

Betsy rubbed her eyes. She put on her woolly bathrobe and her bunny bedroom slippers. Father was waiting for her in the hall. "Be very quiet," said Father, as he opened the door of Mother's room. Mother was in bed. Betsy thought she was asleep.

Father led Betsy over to the corner of the room. There was the white bassinet that had once been Betsy's. Betsy's eyes were very big as she looked into the bassinet, for there lay a tiny baby, sound asleep.

"Oh," whispered Betsy, "is it a baby sister?"

"Yes," whispered Father, "it's a baby sister!"

Betsy couldn't take her eyes off the baby. As

she stood looking at her, she heard some voices far away singing Christmas carols. They were singing a song that Betsy knew.

"Silent night, holy night.
All is calm, all is bright
Round yon Virgin Mother and Child.
Holy infant so tender and mild,
Sleep in heavenly peace. Sleep in heavenly peace."

Betsy tiptoed over to her mother's bed. She leaned over and Mother opened her eyes. She smiled at her little girl.

"Thank you for my present," said Betsy. "Do you hear 'Holy Night,' Mother?"

"Yes, darling," said Mother. "Holy Night."

6

Christmas Star

Betsy had the happiest Christmas day she had ever known. After she saw her baby sister she went downstairs with Father. The house was still quite dark. When they went into the living room, Father pushed the electric light button. Suddenly the room seemed full of twinkling stars. There stood the Christmas tree covered with colored lights and shining balls. Tinsel dripped from the branches like icicles. On the very tip top there was a shining silver star.

Betsy stood in the doorway and looked at the Christmas tree. "Oh!" she sighed; "it's beautiful."

Then she walked over to look at the things that were under the tree. She didn't know what to look at first. Everything seemed to dance before her eyes. She looked around the room to see if there was a bicycle but she didn't see any. There were rollerskates from Aunt Jane, a camera from Granddaddy, a game from Uncle Jim, and a red sweater from Mother, but there wasn't any bicycle. There was a book from Mrs. Beckett.

"Well," said Father. "Aren't you going to see what is in your stocking?"

"Oh, I almost forgot about my stocking," said Betsy.

Betsy went over to the fireplace and Father took down her stocking. It was bulging, and sticking out of the top was a gingerbread boy. Betsy found a lot more presents in her stocking. There were a string of pink beads, a little red pocketbook, a new pencil box, six pencils with her name stamped in gold letters, and a box of

crayons. There were also candies and nuts and a big orange down near the foot. In the very toe of her stocking Betsy found a little silver thimble. She was delighted with this, for Mother was teaching her to sew.

Betsy didn't mind a bit about the bicycle. She guessed that a bicycle and a baby sister would have been too much anyway.

After breakfast Mrs. Beckett let Betsy watch her while she washed and dressed the baby. Betsy wished that she were big enough to wash and dress her. She could hardly keep her hands off her. She loved to touch the baby's cheek, it was so soft.

When the baby was washed and dressed, Mrs. Beckett carried her to her bassinet. "Oh, Mrs. Beckett!" said Betsy, "couldn't I hold her just once?"

"Well, very carefully," said Mrs. Beckett. Betsy held out her arms and Mrs. Beckett put the tiny baby in them. "Oh," said Betsy, "she's the nicest present that ever was. Much nicer than a bicycle."

"Now hand her over," said Mrs. Beckett, as she took the baby again.

When Mrs. Beckett had laid her in the bas-

sinet, she said, "What are you going to name this baby of yours, Betsy?"

"I don't know," said Betsy, walking over to Mother's bed. "It ought to be a Christmasy name, don't you think so, Mother?"

"Oh, yes," said Mother, "a nice Christmasy name."

At dinner Betsy said, "Father, what do you think would be a nice Christmasy name for the baby?"

"Well," said Father, "you might name her Pudding. She certainly looks like one."

"Oh, Father!" cried Betsy. "Pudding would be a terrible name for a little girl."

"Well, you can't call her Turkey because that is the name of a country."

"I wouldn't want to call her Turkey anyway," laughed Betsy. "Of course we could call her Carol after Christmas carol, but I know a lot of Carols. I want her to have a different name."

"How about naming her after one of Santa Claus's reindeer?" said Father. "Let's see; there were Dasher and Dancer, I remember, and Donder and Blitzen. Any one of those would be different."

Betsy laughed so hard she choked on her plum pudding. "Oh, Father, they are awful names for a baby."

"Well," laughed Father, "you will have to think of a name yourself."

In the afternoon Billy came to see Betsy's Christmas tree.

"I have a baby sister," said Betsy the moment she saw Billy.

"That's nothing," said Billy. "I got a two-wheel bike. It's got red wheels."

"My baby sister has a lot of brown curly hair," said Betsy.

"Oh, boy! You ought to see the bell on my bike," said Billy.

"I don't know what to name her," said Betsy.

"My bike is named the Flying Arrow," said Billy.

"I could have had a bicycle," said Betsy, "only I wanted a baby sister."

"You did?" said Billy. "Gee, you must be crazy."

Betsy showed Billy all of her presents. They went out of doors and Betsy took some pictures of Billy and Billy took some of Betsy.

"Say, Betsy," said Billy, "will you take a picture of me on my bike?"

"Maybe," said Betsy.

"Maybe I'll let you ride it, if you will take my picture," said Billy.

The children spent the rest of the afternoon playing a game.

Father kept going to the front door every once in a while. Finally Betsy said, "What are you looking for, Father?"

"Just looking to see if Santa Claus dropped anything outside," said Father.

"Did he?" Betsy asked.

"I haven't found anything," said Father, "but

you never can tell. Sometimes things roll off the
roof."

"Oh, Father!" laughed Betsy. "You're just
teasing."

Late in the afternoon there was a loud ring at
the front door. Father and Betsy and Billy all
rushed to the door. When Father opened it, there
stood a delivery man with a shiny two-wheel
bicycle.

Betsy's eyes looked as though they were going
to pop right out of her head.

"Oh, boy!" shouted Billy; "a two-wheeler, just like mine!"

"Merry Christmas," said the delivery man; "sorry to be so late."

"Merry Christmas," said Father. "I have been looking for you all day. You should get a sleigh and some reindeer. You would get around faster."

"Is it for me, Father?" asked Betsy, putting her hand on one of the beautiful red wheels.

"Yes, Betsy, it is for you," said Father.

"Oh, Father," said Betsy, "a baby sister and a bike, both! It's wonderful!"

That evening Betsy was sitting on Father's lap. He was reading her Christmas book out loud. Betsy listened to every word. After a while she looked up at the Christmas tree. She began at the bottom and looked at each branch. At last her eyes rested on the beautiful silver star on the very top. It seemed to twinkle at her.

"Father," cried Betsy, "I know what I'm going to name the baby."

"What?" said Father.

"I'm going to name her Star," said Betsy.

"Star!" said Father. "Let's go tell Mother."

7

Valentine Hearts

"Mother," cried Betsy, as she rushed in from school one day, "I have to take a quarter of a pound of butter to school tomorrow."

"A quarter of a pound of butter!" said Mother. "What are you going to do with a quarter of a pound of butter?"

"We're going to make cookies," said Betsy. "A very special kind of cookie, only what kind is a secret."

"Where are you going to make the cookies?" asked Mother.

"Oh, in the school kitchen," said Betsy. "All of the children are going to bring something, everything that goes in cookies. Miss Grey said if we each brought a little bit, when we put it all together there would be enough to make a lot of cookies."

"I see," said Mother. "What are you going to do with so many cookies?"

"That's a secret," said Betsy, as she danced out of the room.

Now the secret was that the children were making cookies for their mothers. They were to be Valentine Cookies. Miss Grey was going to bring some cookie cutters shaped like hearts.

Valentine's Day was just two days off. The children had made paper Valentines for each other. Betsy made a red heart for her baby sister. She pasted gold stars all over the heart.

Miss Grey had made a make-believe postbox with a great big red heart on the outside. It was so big that it almost covered the box. As the children finished making their Valentines, they dropped them into the box. Betsy hoped that there would be a lot of Valentines for her when Miss Grey opened the box on Valentine's Day.

When the children had asked Miss Grey if they could make Valentines for their mothers, Miss Grey had said, "How would you like to make Valentine Cookies?" The children were delighted, for they felt that nothing could be nicer than Valentine Cookies.

The next morning Betsy started off to school with her quarter of a pound of butter. Just before she reached the school she met Billy. Billy had a paper bag filled with flour. His mother had wrapped it up carefully and tied it with a string.

Billy was now using the bag of flour for a ball. He was tossing it up in the air and catching it.

"You better watch out," said Betsy, "or you will drop that flour."

"Aw, I'm a good catcher," said Billy, tossing the little package higher than ever.

Just then Billy slipped on some ice on the pavement. Ker-plunk! went Billy and sat down very hard.

Ker-plunk! went the bag of flour, right on the top of Billy's head. The bag burst and the flour went all over Billy. He looked so funny, sitting in the middle of the pavement covered with flour, that Betsy couldn't help laughing.

Billy rubbed the flour out of his eyes. "Gee!" he said, "I slipped."

He scrambled to his feet and tried to brush the flour off of his suit. When he finished, the white flour was smeared all over him. Then he pulled off his hat and the flour got all over his hair.

When he reached his classroom, Miss Grey said, "Why, Billy, is it snowing outside?"

"Billy was playing ball with his bag of flour," said Betsy.

"I slipped and it hit me on the head," said Billy.

"Oh, Billy!" said Miss Grey, "now you have wasted the flour for the cookies."

Billy looked down at himself. He was a sight! "Can't I have any of the cookies, Miss Grey?" he asked.

"Well, you will have to stay after school and wash the pots and pans all by yourself. It was very careless of you to lose the flour," said Miss Grey.

Toward the end of the morning, Miss Grey took the children up to the school kitchen. It was on the top floor of the school. In the kitchen there was a long table, a stove, a cupboard, and a sink. The children had never been in the kitchen before and they thought it was a wonderful place.

Miss Grey opened the doors of the cupboard. She took out some little bowls and a great big bowl. She took out some flat cookie tins, a flour sifter, and an eggbeater. She laid everything on the table.

"Have you got the cookie cutters?" asked Betty Jane.

"Yes," answered Miss Grey, "here they are." Miss Grey handed Betty Jane a paper bag and Betty Jane took six heart-shaped cookie cutters out of the bag.

Chris-topher came in with a big bottle of milk that the milk-man had left with the jan-itor.

Soon everyone was busy. Betty Jane sifted the flour. El-len beat the eggs. Betsy

mixed the butter and sugar together. Christopher and Kenny greased the tins. Billy lit the oven. Mary Lou measured the baking powder and Richard measured the salt. The rest of the chil-dren sprinkled a little flour on the long wooden table so that they would be all ready to roll out the dough.

Everything had to be added to Betsy's bowl of butter and sugar, so she mixed and mixed. She had to make the dough very smooth.

All of the children crowded around Betsy.

At last Miss Grey said that the dough was ready to be rolled. She gave each of the children who had floured the table a piece of dough. As there were only three rolling pins, the children had to take turns.

"Look out there, Billy!" said Miss Grey; "don't roll it too thin."

"Miss Grey, it's sticking to my rolling pin," said Henry.

"Can I begin to cut mine?" asked a new little girl named Sally.

Six of the children began to cut the cookies. Ellen and Christopher lifted the hearts off of the table and placed them on the flat tins. Betsy

sprinkled a little sugar on them and Kenny put the pans in the oven.

It didn't take very long for the cookies to bake. Just as soon as one pan had turned a beautiful golden color, another pan was ready to go into the oven. Pan after pan went into the oven and came out to cool on the table. When the cookies were cool, the children helped to take them off of the tins. When they were all laid out on a white cloth, there were over one hundred cookies. Some of the hearts were a little crooked but any mother could tell that they were hearts. Some of them were broken and Miss Grey said that the children could eat the broken pieces. How they gobbled them down!

"Oh, boy!" said Billy, with his mouth full of cookie; "I thought I was going to bust if I didn't get a taste of those cookies."

"Burst, Billy," said Miss Grey, "not bust."

Miss Grey took a big tin can out of the cupboard. "Now," she said, "we will put them in this big can to keep overnight. Tomorrow we will divide them and wrap them up in red tissue paper. Then you can take them home for mother's Valentine."

The next day the children were terribly excited. When Miss Grey opened the postbox, there were Valentines for every child in the room. Betsy received ten and she was delighted with every one.

At recess time Miss Grey sent Kenny up to the kitchen to get the can of cookies. In about five minutes Kenny returned. "I can't find any can, Miss Grey," said Kenny.

"Oh, Kenny!" said Miss Grey; "I left it on the table, right by the door. Betsy, you go with Kenny. Perhaps you can help him to find the can."

Betsy and Kenny climbed up to the third floor. They went into the kitchen. There was no can in sight. The children opened the lower doors of the cupboard. There was nothing there but tin pans.

"Maybe it is up top," said Kenny. Betsy climbed on a chair and opened the closet doors but there was no can there. They looked under the table and back of the stove. The can of cookies was gone.

Betsy and Kenny went downstairs. When they told Miss Grey that the cookies were gone, she couldn't believe it. But when Miss Grey looked everywhere in the kitchen, she knew that the children were right.

Miss Grey asked the janitor, Mr. Windrim, if he had seen the can of cookies, but he didn't know anything about them. She asked the principal of the school and all of the teachers, but no one knew anything about the cookies.

When Miss Grey told the children that their cookies were lost they almost cried. Their lovely cookies that they had baked especially for their mothers' Valentines! They were gone and no one knew where.

Miss Grey tried to have a singing lesson but the children sang very badly. They were all thinking about the lost cookies.

After a while, Billy raised his hand.

"What is it, Billy?" asked Miss Grey.

"May I get a drink?" asked Billy.

"Do you have to have a drink of water now, Billy?" asked Miss Grey. "You know you have just had your recess."

"I'm awful thirsty," said Billy.

"Very well," said Miss Grey, "but hurry back."

Billy ran out to the drinking fountain in the yard. The ash-men were collecting the big cans of rubbish that were standing on the school pavement. They were throwing the cans up into the wagon. Just as Billy was about to get a drink, he saw one of the men pick up a can with a lid on it.

"Hey! Hey!" cried Billy, rushing toward the man. "Hey! Wait a minute."

The man put the can down on the pavement and looked at Billy. "What's the matter with you?" he said.

"Hey!" said Billy, "that's our cookies."

Billy picked up the can and ran into school. When he rushed into the room carrying the cookie can, the children shouted, "Look what Billy's got!"

"I found the cookies, Miss Grey. I found 'em!"

cried Billy. "Somebody must have put them out on the pavement with the rubbish. The man was just going to take them away."

Billy was all out of breath but the children were delighted to have the cookies back again.

Just then Mr. Windrim came into the room. "Miss Grey," he said, "I am terribly sorry about those cookies. The boy who helps me with the cleaning made a mistake and put your can out with the rubbish. Now I am afraid it is gone."

"No, Mr. Windrim, Billy rescued the can of cookies just as the men were about to take it."

"Gee, Miss Grey!" said Billy, "aren't you glad I had to get a drink of water?"

"Indeed I am," said Miss Grey.

"Oh, Miss Grey!" cried Billy, "I forgot to get it. Now what do you think of that!"

8

Thumpy Goes for a Ride

Thumpy was Betsy's little dog. He was a black cocker spaniel and Betsy had raised him from a tiny puppy. He was a loving little fellow and a good watchdog but he had one very bad habit. He stole everything he could find to eat and he didn't seem to be one bit ashamed of himself.

Once he climbed on a chair and knocked a box of chocolates off of the living room table. When the chocolates rolled out of the box, Thumpy gobbled them all up. Betsy walked into the room just as Thumpy was tearing the box to pieces. He didn't want to miss any crumbs.

Another time the refrigerator door was left open on a crack. When Thumpy found himself alone in the kitchen he poked his nose in the crack and the door swung open. Thumpy sniffed here and he sniffed there. Then he poked the lid off of a dish filled with stewed chicken. When Betsy's mother came into the kitchen, Thumpy was curled up on a chair, sound asleep. When Mother looked into the refrigerator there wasn't even a chicken bone left in the dish.

Of course Thumpy was punished each time but it didn't seem to do any good. He just went right on gobbling down everything he could find and he didn't seem to mind being sick at his tummy.

Father said that Thumpy's motto was, "Eats! Eats! and more Eats!"

One afternoon Mother came home with some chopped meat for dinner. She laid the package in the center of the kitchen table and went upstairs to see if the baby was awake. In a few minutes she hurried down to prepare dinner. It was late and Father would soon be home. When she pushed open the kitchen door, what did she find but Thumpy standing in the center of the table. He was just finishing off the last bit of meat. "Thumpy!" cried Mother. "You naughty, naughty boy!"

Betsy came running from the playroom. "What did he do?" she cried.

"He has eaten all of the meat for dinner," said Mother.

"Oh, Thumpy!" cried Betsy. "Shame on you! Stealing Mother's meat!"

Thumpy put on a long face and his ears seemed to hang down longer than ever.

"Are you going to whip him, Mother?" asked Betsy.

"Indeed I am," replied Mother. Mother whipped Thumpy with a newspaper and put him outside.

Just then Father came home. Betsy ran to meet him. "Father!" she called. "Thumpy just ate up our dinner."

"He did?" said Father. "Well, let us eat Thumpy's."

"We can't eat Thumpy's," said Betsy. "Thumpy's dinner comes in a can with ground bones in it."

"Where is he now?" asked Father.

"Oh, Mother whipped him and put him out of doors," said Betsy.

"Well, he better not get outside of the gate," said Father. "The dogcatchers are around."

"It would just serve Thumpy right if the dogcatchers got him," said Betsy. "He's a very naughty boy."

"I don't suppose you would go after Thumpy if the dogcatchers caught him, would you?" asked Father.

"No, I wouldn't," said Betsy, tossing her braids. "He's a naughty boy and it would serve him right."

That evening Betsy and Father and Mother ate vegetables for their dinner.

The next day was Saturday and Betsy spent the morning making paper dolls. After lunch she started off for Ellen's house. She was going to spend the rest of the day playing with Ellen. As Betsy closed the front door she thought of Thumpy. She hadn't seen anything of him for a long time. Betsy knew that he wasn't in the house so she looked in his kennel. Thumpy wasn't there. Betsy called, "Here, Thumpy! Here, Thump!" but Thumpy didn't appear. Then Betsy looked at the gate. It was wide open. Betsy knew at once that Thumpy was gone. Then she thought of the dogcatchers. Her little heart seemed to stand still, she was so frightened.

Like a flash she was off. "Here, Thumpy! Here, Thumpy!" she called. As she neared the corner she could hear a great deal of barking. Around the corner she flew. Sure enough, there was the dogcatcher's wagon. A man with a big net was chasing a little black cocker spaniel across the street. "Swish!" went the big net right over Thumpy, and Betsy saw her little dog scooped up like a fish.

Betsy ran toward the man with the net, but before she could reach him Thumpy had been tossed into the wire cage on the wagon. The cage was packed with wriggling, squealing, barking dogs.

"Stop! Stop! Stop!" shrieked Betsy. "Don't take Thumpy away!"

The man paid no attention to Betsy. He jumped on the back of the wagon and away it went with all of the dogs.

Betsy ran after the wagon as fast as her legs could carry her. She could see Thumpy looking out of the wire cage. Tears ran down her cheeks and her legs grew very tired but on and on she ran. The wagon was getting farther and farther away. Thumpy looked like a black spot now. Betsy tried to run faster but her breath was giving out. She had to keep running. She couldn't stop now. They were taking her little Thumpy away. Her precious Thumpy!

Just then the dogcatcher's wagon disappeared over a hill. Betsy sat down on a step and put her head down on her arm. She cried and cried and cried. She was so tired from running and she had lost Thumpy after all. Betsy was still sobbing when a bright red automobile stopped beside her. "I say, Little Red Ribbons!" shouted the man in the automobile. "What's the trouble?"

Betsy looked up. There was Mr. Kilpatrick sitting at the wheel of the automobile.

"Oh, Mr. Kilpatrick!" cried Betsy, "the dog-catchers have taken Thumpy. They went over that hill with Thumpy and now I'll never see him again."

"Get in," said Mr. Kilpatrick, opening the door of the car.

Betsy got in. "Now stop crying," said the policeman; "we'll get Thumpy all right."

"Can you make them give Thumpy back to me, Mr. Kilpatrick?" asked Betsy.

"Now there's no use in chasing the wagon," said Mr. Kilpatrick. "The thing to do is to go to the dog pound where they dump them out. We'll wait for them there. It will cost you fifty cents to get Thumpy back. Is he worth fifty cents?"

"Oh, yes, Mr. Kilpatrick," cried Betsy. "I have fifty cents in my bank. I would give all of the money in my bank to get Thumpy back."

"That settles it!" said Mr. Kilpatrick, as he turned the car around. "We'll stop at your house and you can get your money."

When they reached Betsy's house, Betsy jumped out. In a second she was back again. She had her little bank in her hand. "I've got the money," she cried as she climbed into the car.

While Mr. Kilpatrick drove to the dog pound,

Betsy opened her bank with the little key that hung on a chain around her neck. She took out ten nickels.

"You're sure they will give Thumpy back to me for fifty cents, aren't you, Mr. Kilpatrick?" said Betsy.

"Sure as your name is Betsy!" said Mr. Kilpatrick.

The red automobile drove up to the gates of the dog pound just as the dogcatcher's wagon drove through the gates.

"There he is!" cried Betsy. "There's Thumpy!"

Thumpy was still looking out through the wire cage. He looked surprised and very sad. When he saw Betsy, he gave a little bark and wagged his stubby tail.

Mr. Kilpatrick and Betsy got out of the car. They went into a little office. Mr. Kilpatrick told the man in the office that they had come for Betsy's dog.

"Very well," said the man, "come pick him out."

Betsy went out to the wagon and pointed to Thumpy. The man lifted him out of the wire cage and put him on the ground. Thumpy rushed to Betsy. He jumped up and down barking little happy barks. Betsy picked up her little dog and hugged him tight. "Oh, Thumpy!" she cried, "I'm so glad to see you."

"Now you keep him off the street," said the man.

"Oh, I will," replied Betsy, handing over her fifty cents.

Betsy climbed back into Mr. Kilpatrick's car and he drove Betsy and Thumpy home.

"Oh, Mr. Kilpatrick, I don't know what I would do without you."

"Sure," said Mr. Kilpatrick, "I don't know myself what you would do. It was a good thing I came along, just in the nick of time."

"Oh, yes," said Betsy. "Thank you so much."

When Betsy reached home, she told Mother and Father all about Thumpy and the dogcatchers.

"I thought you said that you wouldn't go after Thumpy if the dogcatchers got him," said Father.

Betsy pressed her cheek against Thumpy's silky head. She looked up into Father's eyes. Then Betsy and Father laughed very hard.

"Perhaps Thumpy will be good now," said Betsy.

"Perhaps," said Father, "but I wouldn't trust him with a beefsteak."

9

May Day and Mother Goose

One rainy day in April the children were so wiggly that Miss Grey felt like the "Old Woman That Lived in a Shoe."

"She had so many children, she didn't know what to do."

Christopher had tied Betsy's braids together in a knot twice. Kenny had dropped a marble down the neck of Ellen's dress. Betty Jane cried because Billy untied her sash every time she went to the front of the room to write on the blackboard. Miss Grey tried very hard to teach her second grade how to tell time by the clock. Nobody seemed to care what time it was. They just watched the rain run down the windows in rivers.

At last Miss Grey said, "Let's talk about our May Day. It won't be long until May Day."

The children all sat up and their faces brightened.

"Are we going to have a May Queen?" asked Betsy.

"Yes, indeed," said Miss Grey. "It wouldn't be May Day without a May Queen."

"And a maypole?" asked Mary Lou.

"Yes," said Miss Grey, "but we must plan something more to entertain your mothers and fathers. Let's all put on our thinking caps and see if we can think of something nice to do."

The children sat quietly and thought very hard. Billy thought so hard that his face was wrinkled up like a withered apple. Betsy stared straight ahead with her eyes glued on a picture of Little Bo-Peep. Then she looked at the rest of the Mother Goose pictures that hung above the blackboards. Suddenly Betsy had an idea. She raised her hand.

"Yes, Betsy," said Miss Grey, "have you thought of something?"

Betsy stood up. "I think it would be nice if we dressed up like the Mother Goose children and looked like those pictures over the blackboards."

"Why, Betsy, that is a lovely idea," said Miss Grey. "How many children would like to be Mother Goose children?"

All of the children raised their hands.

"Well, Betsy," said Miss Grey, "it was your idea so you can choose what you would like to be."

"I would like to be Mary Had a Little Lamb," replied Betsy, "because my grandfather has lambs on his farm and he might let me have one to bring to school on May Day."

The rest of the afternoon went very fast indeed. No one looked out of the windows at the rain. No one thought of naughty things to do. Everyone was busy thinking about May Day.

By the time the bell rang for the children to go home everything was settled. Ellen was to be the May Queen because she was the prettiest little girl in the class. Billy wanted to be Tom, Tom, the Piper's Son. Mary Lou wanted to be Mary, Mary, Quite Contrary. Kenny and Sally were to be Jack and Jill. Betty Jane was delighted to be Little Miss Muffet. Richard was to be Little Jack Horner and Henry Little Tommy Tucker. There were enough Mother Goose children to give every child in the class a part. The children went home feeling very happy.

Betsy and Billy walked home together.

"Say, Betsy," said Billy, "do you really think your grandfather will let you have a real live lamb to bring to school?"

"I think so," said Betsy. "I'm going to write him a letter and ask him tonight."

"Gee," said Billy, "I wish I could have a real live pig. I have to say

'Tom, Tom, the piper's son,
Stole a pig and away he run.'

What am I going to have under my arm if I don't have any pig?"

"You could put the wastepaper basket under your arm," said Betsy.

"Aw, say!" said Billy; "who wants a wastepaper basket! I have to have a pig, I tell you. A real live pig."

"My granddaddy has pigs too," said Betsy.

"He has?" said Billy. "Do you think he would let me have a pig?"

"I don't think so," said Betsy.

"Why not?" asked Billy.

"Well, I never heard of anybody borrowing a pig," said Betsy.

"You're going to borrow a lamb, aren't you?" said Billy. "There isn't any difference between a lamb and a pig."

"Oh, yes, there is," laughed Betsy.

"I would take good care of it," said Billy, "and I would give it back to him."

"Well, I'll ask him," said Betsy.

That evening, Betsy wrote to her grandfather on the farm. This is what she wrote:

Dear Grandaddy,
We are going to have a May Day at school. I am to be "Mary Had a Little Lamb" and I need a lamb. Billy Porter is "Tom, Tom the Piper's Son" and he would like to have a pig. A little one will do. We will take good care of them and send them back to you. It rains all the time. I am a good girl.
Love and kisses,
Betsy.

Betsy could hardly wait to receive an answer to her letter. Every morning she ran to meet the mailman at the door. Billy waited at the corner for her every morning. "Did you get the letter?" he would say.

After several days the letter came. Granddaddy's answer was "Yes." Betsy raced up the street to Billy. "Granddaddy says we can have the lamb and the pig," she cried.

"Oh, boy!" shouted Billy. "That's fine! When do we get them?"

"Granddaddy says he'll send them by express in plenty of time," said Betsy.

Billy and Betsy trotted along to school feeling very happy. Soon they met some of the other children.

"What do you think?" said Billy. "I'm going to have a real live pig."

"And I'm going to have a real lamb," said Betsy. "My grandaddy is sending them."

"Well, I could have a real live spider if I wanted one," said Betty Jane, who was to be Little Miss Muffet. "But I don't want a real live spider. My mother is going to make me a big one out of colored paper."

"Aw, you're afraid of spiders," shouted Billy.

"I am not," said Betty Jane.

The children hurried along to school calling out, "Betty Jane's afraid of spiders! Betty Jane's afraid of spiders!"

When they reached Mr. Kilpatrick, Billy shouted, "I'm going to have a pig for May Day, Mr. Kilpatrick."

"Well, see that you hold on to it," said Mr. Kilpatrick. "We don't want any pigs running loose on the highway."

Two days before the first of May the express-man drove up to Betsy's door and left two wooden crates. Inside of the crates were the little white lamb and the little pink pig.

Betsy's father had fenced off a part of the yard with chicken wire. There Betsy put the lamb and the pig. Betsy loved the little lamb. It was so gentle and it sounded a little bit sad when it said "Baa." She petted it and pulled up handfuls of grass for it to eat.

Billy spent all of his time at Betsy's looking at his pig. It was a little bit hard to hold and it squealed most of the time, but Billy was very gentle with it.

At last May Day arrived. Betsy was up bright and early and Billy arrived long before breakfast.

They were both wearing their costumes. Billy wore a Scottish kilt and Betsy wore a long pink dress with a hoop skirt and ruffled pantalettes.

Betsy's father put the pig and the lamb into the crates. Then he put the crates in the automobile. Billy and Betsy and Betsy's mother got in the car and they all drove to the school.

It was a beautiful day and the maypole looked very gay with the bright ribbons blowing in the breeze. Mr. Windrim had put the pole in the center of the playground across the street from the school. Near the pole he had built a platform. Then he had made a throne for the May Queen. When all of the fathers and mothers were seated on the chairs around the platform, Ellen walked out and took her seat on the throne. Sally put a wreath of flowers on her head while all of the children sang a Spring Song. Then the children took hold of the ribbons and danced around the maypole.

After the maypole dance was over the children gave their Mother Goose performance. When Betsy's turn came, she lifted the lamb out of the crate. She put it down on the ground and coaxed it very softly. The little lamb said, "Baa!" and wandered off. Betsy went after it. "Come, come,

Baby," she coaxed, but the lamb wouldn't follow Betsy.

Everyone was waiting for Betsy to appear, but the lamb would not budge a step. "You will have to carry it," said Miss Grey.

Betsy picked up the lamb and carried it out onto the platform. As she held it in her arms, she said,

> "Mary had a little lamb
>   With fleece as white as snow,
>   And everywhere that Mary went
>   The lamb was sure to go."

Just then the lamb began to go, for it slipped lower and lower in Betsy's arms.

Betsy went on:

> "It followed her to school one day,
>   That was against the rule;
>   It made the children laugh and play
>   To see a lamb at school."

"Baa! Baa!" said the lamb. Betsy took a deep breath.

"And so the teacher turned it out,
But still it lingered near,
And waited patiently about
Till Mary did appear."

By this time the lamb had slipped so low that Betsy decided to put it down. She thought it would be better if she sat down too, so she squatted down beside the lamb and finished her piece.

" 'Why does the lamb love Mary so?'
The eager children cry.
'Why, Mary loves the lamb, you know!'
The teacher did reply."

Everyone clapped as Betsy led the lamb away. Then it was Billy's turn. Billy picked up his pig and tucked it under his arm. He ran out on the platform and said in a very loud voice,

"Tom, Tom, the piper's son,
Stole a pig and away he run."

Just then the pig slipped from under Billy's arm. It dropped to the ground and away it ran as fast as it could go. Billy jumped down from the platform and raced after the pig. It flew across the green grass and down the street. Billy sped after it.

Mr. Kilpatrick was standing in the center of the big wide street. Just as he blew his whistle, he looked up the street. He saw the little pig coming towards him and Billy pounding along behind the pig. The pig was making straight for Mr. Kilpatrick. The big policeman stooped down and caught it just like a football. Billy was all out of breath when he reached Mr. Kilpatrick.

"Didn't I tell you not to let this pig get away?"
said Mr. Kilpatrick, as he handed the pig to
Billy. "Haven't I got enough to do without having
to catch runaway pigs?"

"Oh, gee, Mr. Kilpatrick, I couldn't help it,"
said Billy, "it slipped."

10

The Wishing Well

The week before school closed was the busiest week that Betsy had ever known. All of the children were as busy as bees. In every room they hammered and sawed and painted and pasted. Rolls and rolls of brightly colored crepe paper were piled up on tables. The whole school was getting ready for a bazaar.

At first the children in the second grade didn't

know what a bazaar was. Billy said he thought
he had seen one at the zoo.

Miss Grey said, "No, Billy, a bazaar is not
an animal."

Betsy said that she had been to a bazaar once.
"They had tables trimmed with pretty colored
paper," she said. "And they sold all kinds of
things. They sold cakes and dolls and flowers

and preserves and everything you could think of."

"When are we going to have the bazaar?" asked Kenny.

"The last day of school," said Miss Grey.

"And are we going to sell things?" asked Billy.

"Yes, Billy," answered Miss Grey.

"What will we do with all of the money?" said Billy.

"The money is going to be spent for new things for our school playground," said Miss Grey. "It will buy a new sliding board, some new basketballs, a football, baseballs, and bats. Of course it depends upon how much money we earn."

"What will the second grade sell?" asked Ellen.

"I haven't decided yet," said Miss Grey.

Betsy raised her hand. "Yes, Betsy," said Miss Grey.

"At the bazaar that I went to, they had a wishing well. You put ten cents in the bucket and when the bucket came up there was a surprise package in it. It was fun. I got my bank in the wishing well."

"Couldn't we have a wishing well?" asked Kenny.

"I believe we could, Kenny," said Miss Grey, "but we would have to build it ourselves."

The children thought it would be wonderful to have a wishing well. Christopher said that his father had a grocery store and that he could get a big sugar barrel to make the wishing well.

A week before the bazaar Christopher and Billy brought the sugar barrel to school in an express wagon. The children set to work at once. They cut a big piece out of the side of the barrel

down near the bottom. This made an opening where someone could reach in and put the surprises in the bucket. They covered the rest of the barrel with large sheets of paper. With gray and white and black paint they made the paper look like stones. Across the top of the barrel they fastened a rod with a handle. Billy tied the bucket on the end of a piece of rope. Then he tied the rope to the center of the rod.

"Now let's turn the handle and see if it works," said Kenny.

Betsy turned the handle. Down went the bucket to the bottom of the well. She turned it again and the bucket came up.

"It works, Miss Grey!" the children shouted.

"Splendid!" said Miss Grey. "You have made a wonderful well. Now I hope we will have a lot of nice surprise packages to put in the bucket."

The children could hardly wait until the last day of school. It was the day for the bazaar and the day they would be promoted to the third grade.

When the day came, Miss Grey's desk was piled high with little packages. Just before Mr. Windrim came in to carry the wishing well out to the playground, Miss Grey said, "Now, boys and girls, I have some good news for you."

All of the children looked at Miss Grey.

"Every boy and girl in this class is promoted to the third grade," said Miss Grey.

The children clapped their hands. They were so glad that they were all promoted.

"Who is promoted number one?" asked Billy.

"You will have to ask the wishing well," said Miss Grey. "Christopher, will you come and grind up the bucket? The name of the number one child is in the bucket."

The children were very still as Christopher walked to the front of the room. Betsy could feel her heart beat just a little bit faster. She was sure that her name was in the bucket. She had been promoted number one from the first grade. *Of course I will be number one again,* thought Betsy.

Christopher was standing by the wishing well now. He turned the handle very slowly. In a few moments the bucket appeared. Christopher put his hand in the bucket and pulled out a piece of paper. He looked at the paper. Betsy stared straight at Christopher and her eyes were big and round.

"Will you read it, Christopher?" said Miss Grey.

This is what Christopher read: "Ellen is promoted number one."

Betsy could hardly believe her ears. She had been so sure that Christopher would read her name. But he hadn't. Ellen was promoted number one. Betsy looked at Ellen. Her face was

shining, she was so happy. A big lump came up in Betsy's throat. She bit her lip and blinked her eyes to keep back the tears.

Miss Grey looked at Betsy and said, "Betsy, would you like to take charge of the wishing well this afternoon?"

Betsy shook her head. "No," she whispered. Betsy was so disappointed that she didn't even care about the bazaar.

"Well then, I'll do it," said Miss Grey. "Perhaps you will come and help me." Betsy just shook her head.

"Billy and Kenny are going to put the packages in the bucket," said Miss Grey.

Mr. Windrim came in and carried the wishing well out to the playground. He put it in front of some bushes. Billy and Kenny put all of the packages in the bottom of the well. Then they sat down under the bushes to wait for customers.

The playground looked very gay. Each class had a table. The tables were covered with different colored papers. The third grade had made a little house called a Jelly House. They had tiny jars of jelly to sell.

Betsy was feeling so unhappy that she didn't see how pretty the bazaar was. She wished that she could go home but she had promised to meet Mother at the flagpole. She wondered what Mother and Father would say when they heard that she was not promoted number one. She guessed that they would be disappointed in her.

Betsy stood by the flagpole looking very sad. After a while she saw Mother coming towards her. Betsy ran to meet her. She flung her arms around her mother's waist. "Mother, Mother," she cried, "I didn't get promoted number one."

Mother stooped down and put her arms around Betsy. "Come," said Mother, "let's sit down on this bench." Betsy sat down beside Mother. She put her head on Mother's shoulder and cried very hard. "I didn't get promoted number one," she sobbed. "Ellen was promoted number one. I don't like Ellen anymore."

"Now, Betsy," said Mother, "it is not like you to say that and I know that you don't mean it."

Betsy reached for Mother's handkerchief.

"You were promoted, weren't you, Betsy?" said Mother.

"Yes, but I wanted to be first," said Betsy, "just like last year."

Mother patted her little girl's shoulder. "You did the very best you could," she said. "That makes Father and me very happy. It doesn't matter if you were not first. You see, darling, if you were promoted number one all of the time, no one else would know how nice it is to be number one. You like sharing your toys with Ellen and now you are sharing this happiness with her."

Betsy sat up and wiped her eyes. She was beginning to feel a little better. "Then it doesn't matter, does it, Mother?" she said.

"It doesn't matter at all," said Mother. "Shall we take Ellen with us to Grandfather's for the summer?"

"Oh, yes," said Betsy, as she wiped the last tear away. "You will have three little girls this summer, won't you, Mother? You will have Ellen and Star and me."

"Yes," said Mother; "it will be lovely to have three little girls."

Betsy got down off of the bench. "Well now, I have to help Miss Grey with the wishing well," she said.

Betsy and Mother walked over to the wishing well. "I'll help you, Miss Grey," said Betsy.

"Oh, thank you, Betsy," said Miss Grey. "You are just the one I need. Billy and Kenny are

having such a good time putting the packages in the bucket."

Betsy looked down into the well. She could see Billy's bright face peeping up through the opening in the side of the barrel. "We're making a lot of money," said Billy.

"Mother," said Betsy, "I want to whisper something to you."

Mother leaned over and Betsy stood on her tiptoes. "Mother," she said, "wouldn't you like to have a little boy too?"

"A little boy?" said Mother.

"Yes," said Betsy, "couldn't we take Billy too? There is plenty of room at Granddaddy's."

"Perhaps we can," whispered Mother. "We'll see."

Other books in the Odyssey series:

Carolyn Haywood
- ☐ "B" IS FOR BETSY
- ☐ BETSY AND BILLY
- ☐ BACK TO SCHOOL WITH BETSY
- ☐ BETSY AND THE BOYS

Carol Kendall
- ☐ THE GAMMAGE CUP

Eleanor Estes
- ☐ GINGER PYE

Virginia Sorensen
- ☐ MIRACLES ON MAPLE HILL

Henry Winterfeld
- ☐ DETECTIVES IN TOGAS
- ☐ MYSTERY OF THE ROMAN RANSOM

Carl Sandburg
- ☐ ROOTABAGA STORIES, PART ONE
- ☐ ROOTABAGA STORIES, PART TWO

Mary Norton
- ☐ BED-KNOB AND BROOMSTICK
- ☐ THE BORROWERS
- ☐ THE BORROWERS AFIELD
- ☐ THE BORROWERS AFLOAT

Edward Eager
- ☐ HALF MAGIC
- ☐ KNIGHT'S CASTLE
- ☐ MAGIC BY THE LAKE
- ☐ MAGIC OR NOT?
- ☐ SEVEN-DAY MAGIC
- ☐ THE TIME GARDEN
- ☐ THE WELL-WISHERS

Look for these titles and others in the Odyssey series in your local bookstore.

Or send payment in the form of a check or money order to: HBJ (Operator J), 465 S. Lincoln Drive, Troy, Missouri 63379.

Or call: 1-800-543-1918 (ask for Operator J).

☐ I've enclosed my check payable to Harcourt Brace Jovanovich.

Charge my: ☐ Visa ☐ MasterCard ☐ American Express.

Card Expiration Date
_____

Card #

_____
Signature

_____
Name

_____
Address

_____
City   State   Zip

Please send me _____ copy/copies @ $3.95 each.

($3.95 x no. of copies) $ _____

Subtotal $ _____

Your state sales tax   + $ _____

Shipping and handling   + $ _____
($1.50 x no. of copies)

Total $ _____

PRICES SUBJECT TO CHANGE